On with the Show!

Don't miss any of the *paw*fectly fun books in the **PET HOTEL** series!

#1: Calling All Pets!
#2: A Big Surprise
#3: A Nose for Trouble
#4: On with the Show!

PET HOTEL

On with the Show!

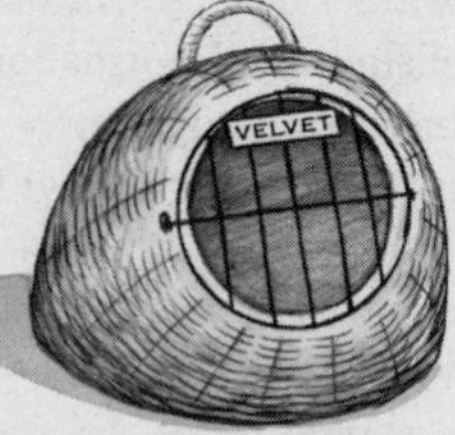

by Kate Finch

illustrated by
John Steven Gurney

SCHOLASTIC INC.

Special thanks to Jane Clarke

For Janice, a great friend and pet-sitter.

ISBN 978-0-545-50184-2

12 11 10 9 8 7 6 5 4 3 2 1 14 15 16 17 18 19/0

Printed in the U.S.A. 40
First printing, January 2014

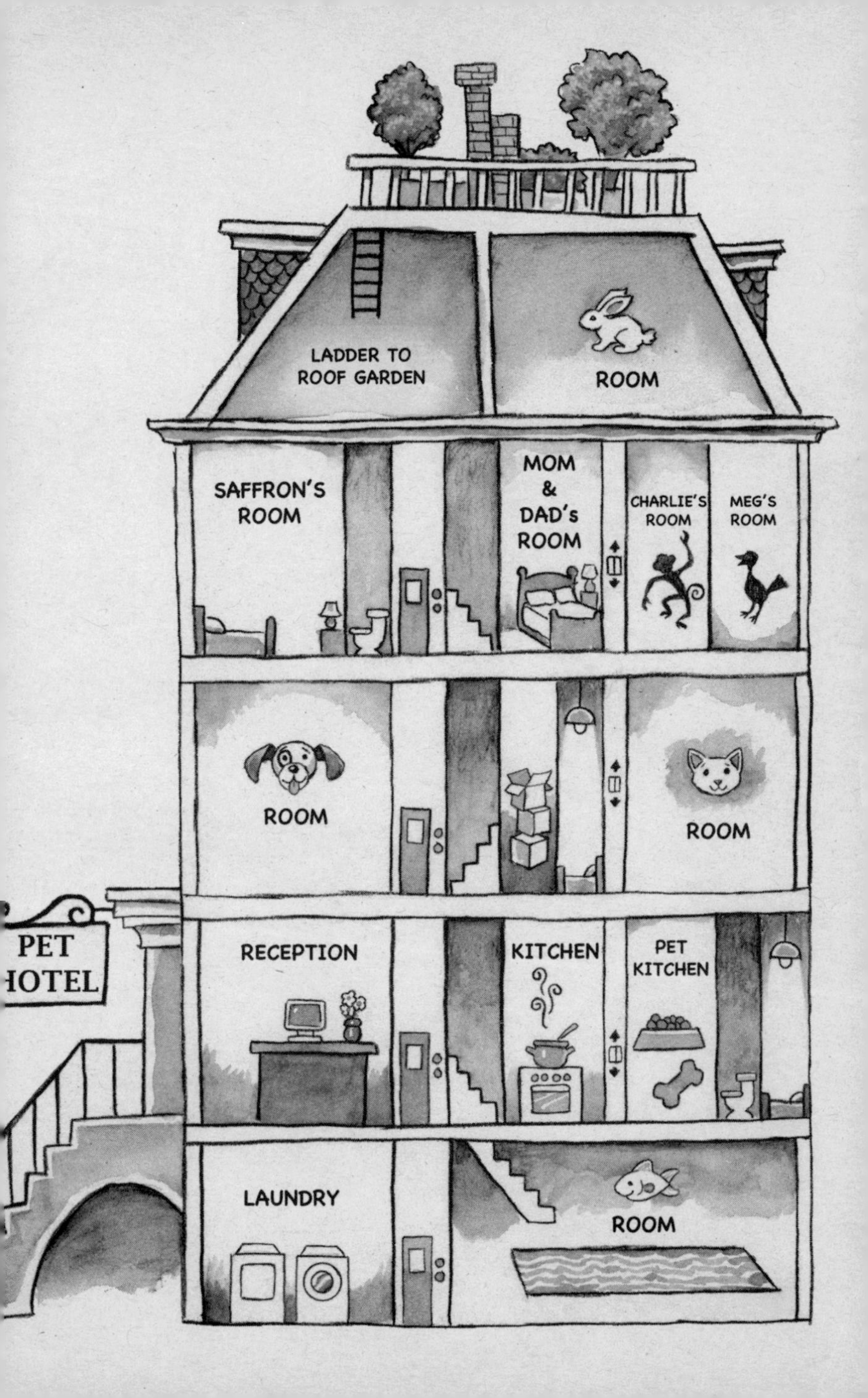
LADDER TO
ROOF GARDEN
ROOM
SAFFRON'S
ROOM
MOM
&
DAD's
ROOM
CHARLIE'S
ROOM
MEG'S
ROOM
ROOM
ROOM
PET
HOTEL
RECEPTION
KITCHEN
PET
KITCHEN
LAUNDRY
ROOM

"It's here, it's here!" Charlie yelled, throwing open the front door of Pet Hotel. Parked right outside was a very long, shiny black car. The driver stepped out and held open the door. She was wearing a gray suit, a sleek hat, and large sunglasses.

"We get to ride in that?" asked Meg, Charlie's twin sister. "Amazing!"

"Wait for me," their great-great-aunt Saffron called as she followed the twins down to the sidewalk. The driver took Saffron's arm and helped her into the car. Little mirrors sewn into her long sunshine-yellow dress flashed and the bells on her earrings jingled as she settled herself into the white leather seat. Meg and Charlie sat on either side of Saffron and buckled their seat belts. They were wearing their best jeans and new matching T-shirts that read PET HOTEL above a cute drawing of Buster, who was Meg's puppy, and Woody, who was Charlie's kitten.

"I feel like a celebrity!" Saffron murmured, patting her silver hair and throwing a purple feather boa around her wrinkly neck.

The twins giggled. They were bursting with excitement. A movie star's pet was coming to stay at Pet Hotel — and the limo was taking them to collect their new guest.

Meg and Charlie gazed out of the tinted windows as they drove past Gazebo Square. The huge car had to move slowly because the market was packed with people bustling around brightly-colored food stalls.

Charlie lowered the window when they reached their friend Juan's Cocina Mexicana stand. The delicious scent of limes and chillies wafted into the car. Juan was standing underneath the stall's green-and-white-striped canopy.

"Hey, Juan!" Charlie called. "Look at us! We're in a limo!"

When Juan spotted them, his mouth dropped open.

"*Hola*, my friends!" he called with a chuckle, bending to pick up his puppy, Paco.

Charlie and Meg leaned out the windows, grinning and waving as the limo turned onto Park Street. Juan held up Paco's paw and wiggled it, so it looked like he was waving back.

The driver threaded her way through the busy city and finally pulled up to a tall apartment building that backed onto a beautiful park.

"This is very fancy!" Saffron exclaimed, pointing to the golden canopy over the entrance. A doorman in a dark suit and cap hurried to help them exit the limo.

"Miss Penigree is expecting you," the doorman said as he ushered them through the glass door into a marble-lined hall. "Take the elevator to the penthouse apartment on the thirty-third floor."

He pressed a button in the elevator and stood back so the twins and Saffron could step inside. The doors closed, and they were whisked up to the penthouse.

"This is a zillion times faster than our clunky old elevator at Pet Hotel," Meg said.

"Miss Penigree must be very rich to live here," Charlie declared.

"My dears, Miss Penigree was a huge star in the 1960s," Saffron explained. "She was in *Moonlight Mystery*, *Romance on the River*, and *Follow the Sun*." Saffron sighed. "I loved her in that. So wild and carefree! I hope she hasn't changed."

The elevator doors slid open to reveal the penthouse apartment. A butler wearing an old-fashioned black bow tie and white gloves was waiting for them. He looked down his nose at Meg's and Charlie's jeans and T-shirts.

"You must be here to pick up Velvet, Miss Penigree's pet," he said.

Meg, Charlie, and Saffron exchanged disappointed glances. Maybe they weren't going to meet Miss Penigree after all.

But then a loud, clear voice rang out above them.

"One moment!" An elderly woman wearing a cream-colored silk dressing gown swept down the grand marble staircase next to the elevator. Her frosty silver hair was piled neatly on top of her head and fixed with sparkling diamond pins.

"Miss Penigree!" Saffron breathed.

The movie star regarded them sternly.

"I need to make a few rules clear," she announced. "Velvet is a pedigree Persian show cat and must be kept spotlessly clean. I must insist that you always, always, ALWAYS wash your hands before touching Velvet. My cat is a perfect example of the breed and MUST be ready for the Celebrity Pet Show when I return from the awards ceremony in Los Angeles!"

Meg and Charlie exchanged a nervous glance. Would they be able to take care of a movie star's pet?

Miss Penigree led the twins and Saffron inside her apartment. Meg gasped at the huge oil paintings on the walls and Charlie gazed up at the chandelier glittering near the ceiling.

"It's time you met Velvet," Miss Penigree said. "But first, as I said . . ." She clapped her hands and indicated the bathroom. They trooped in one after the other.

“I like the gold statue by the sink,” Charlie told Miss Penigree when he came out again.

“Statue? That’s not just any statue,” Miss Penigree informed him.

“It’s the top award for acting,” Saffron explained. “Miss Penigree won it for *Follow the Sun*. I loved you in that,” she told the movie star.

"Thank you. It was my finest hour." Miss Penigree sighed. "Now, please show me your hands."

Charlie, Meg, and Saffron reluctantly held out their palms for inspection. Miss Penigree examined their hands carefully and nodded approvingly.

"Follow me to Velvet's bedroom." Miss Penigree strode off down a red-carpeted hallway lined with black-and-white photos.

"There she is in *Romance on the River*," Saffron whispered, pointing out a picture of a young Miss Penigree wearing a safari hat. Another photo showed a glamorous middle-aged woman in a sequined evening gown. "That's Miss Penigree accepting her Oscar," Aunt Saffron explained.

Miss Penigree carefully opened a door.

The twins blinked. Everything in the room was white, including a cat-sized four-poster bed with heart-shaped pillows and a quilted comforter. On top of the bed, a large white cat with long, downy fur was curled up, fast asleep.

"Wake up, Velvet, darling!" Miss Penigree gently stroked her pet's round head. The cat sat up, revealing a crumpled-looking face with a tiny pink snub nose and silvery whiskers. Then the cat opened its eyes. They were sapphire blue and as sparkly as Miss Penigree's diamonds.

"She's very pretty," Charlie said.

"She?" Miss Penigree said with a gasp. "Velvet is a boy!"

"I mean, *he's* a very handsome cat," Charlie quickly corrected himself as Velvet

yawned, showing his sparkling white teeth and pink tongue. "I love cats. I have a kitten named Woody."

"Oh. How delightful," Miss Penigree murmured.

"Madam?" The butler stood in the doorway, clutching a quilted bag covered in pictures of pastel-colored kittens. "I have put together some essentials for Master Velvet."

"Are you sure you packed his favorite toy?" Miss Penigree asked.

"I am." The butler pulled out a tassel made of silver ribbons and wiggled it across Velvet's bedding. The big, fluffy cat leaped to his feet. The butler bounced the toy up and down in front of his snub nose. Velvet batted it to and fro with his snowy paws.

The twins smiled at each other.

"Taking care of Velvet will be fun!" Meg grinned.

Miss Penigree gave her a stern look.

"The important thing is that Velvet is kept spotless!" she reminded them.

The butler replaced the toy in the bag, which he handed to Charlie.

"Master Velvet's grooming equipment is in there, along with cans of his special food," he said. "He travels in this." The butler reached for a white wicker carrier on a shelf.

Miss Penigree kissed Velvet on the nose and popped him onto the satin cushion inside the cat carrier before shutting the door. There was a little silver plaque in the middle of it with VELVET engraved on it. Miss Penigree handed the carrier to Saffron.

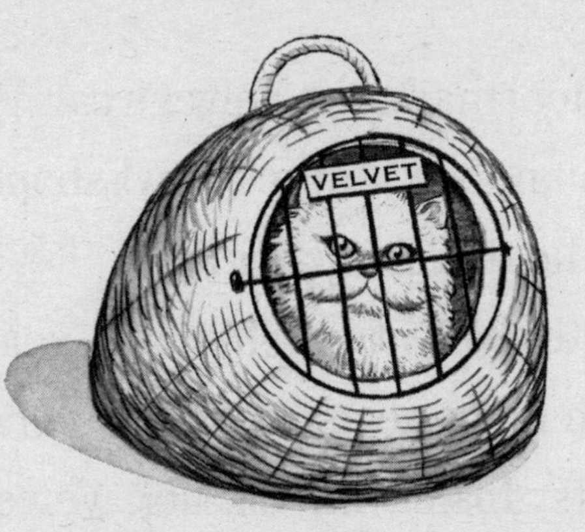

"Remember," she told them as they made their way to the elevator, "Velvet is a pedigree Persian and MUST be kept clean and show-ready!"

"Yes, Miss Penigree!" they all chorused. The elevator doors closed.

Saffron breathed a sigh of relief as they whooshed back down to the ground floor. "Oh, dear," she murmured. "I had no idea that Miss Penigree would be so particular about her cat."

The doorman took Velvet's carrier out to the limo and set it into a bowl-shaped shelf behind the driver's partition.

"Master Velvet has his own seat," Meg said with a giggle as they all fastened their seat belts. Inside his carrier, Velvet rolled over and began to purr.

"It will be easy to take care of Velvet," Charlie said confidently.

"It will," Meg agreed. "As long as he isn't as fussy as his owner!"

"Oh, good, you're back!" the twins' mom said as she opened the door of Pet Hotel. She looked frazzled, and her hair was all over the place. Dad rushed downstairs, panting.

"All the gerbils escaped!" he explained. "We think Pinto opened his cage, then let the others out. We had to chase them all over the hotel."

Meg and Charlie chuckled. Pinto's owner had told them he was an escapologist.

"It's been chaos — the kitchen sink overflowed, the phone's been ringing constantly, and a guide animal just arrived." Mom pushed her hair out of her eyes. "It took forever to round up the gerbils, but we managed to find all of them."

"Then who's that?" Charlie pointed to a honey-colored gerbil on the top shelf of the tall bookcase behind Mom. He was sitting on his hind legs, nibbling at the piece of paper he held in his little pink paws. Meg recognized him at once.

"Pinto!" she exclaimed. "He's got a brown mark around his eye, like Buster's pirate patch."

"He must have gotten out again!" Mom groaned. "Pinto! Stop eating my books!" She tried to grab the gerbil, but the shelf was too high.

"I'll get a stepladder," said Dad with a sigh. He hurried back upstairs.

"My dears," Saffron said to Meg and Charlie. "Why don't you settle Velvet in the Egyptian room while your mom and dad deal with the gerbil situation? I'll make a nice soothing pot of herbal tea." She handed Velvet's carrier to Meg.

"You'll LOVE it here, Velvet," Meg murmured as she took the cat carrier upstairs, into the room that had been turned into a kitty dormitory with pens for six guests. "It's like a film set!" Meg held up the carrier so Velvet could see the statues of pharaohs and the palm trees on the wallpaper.

Four cats skittered up to the fronts of their pens. Charlie stuck his finger through the wires to tickle the ears of each feline guest.

"Hello, Tiger, Jingles, Maggie, and Basil," he murmured. "And hello, Woody!" Charlie turned and whispered to his very own little black-and-white kitten. Woody was fast asleep in his basket by the fireplace, his whiskers twitching and his tail curled over his pink nose.

Meg put Velvet's carrier down in an empty pen and opened the little door. Tiger watched curiously from her pen, blinking her emerald eyes. When Velvet cautiously peeked out of his carrier, Tiger began to purr in delight.

Meg smiled. "Tiger wants to play."

"I'll let her out." Charlie opened Tiger's pen and picked up the big, friendly ginger cat.

"Here's a new friend," Charlie murmured, setting Tiger down so she could see Velvet.

Meg took Velvet's favorite tassel toy out of the bag and dangled it in front of the carrier. The pedigree Persian reached out a perfectly clean white paw to bat the wiggly ribbons.

Tiger's stripy tail twitched and she pounced on the toy with a joyful meow.

"Yeeeow!" Velvet cried in alarm and pulled his paw back into his carrier.

Meg wiggled the toy along the floor to try to tempt him out. Tiger batted at it excitedly.

"Meeeeowww!" Velvet meowed sadly. The twins peered into the carrier. Velvet's fur stood up as if he'd been electrified.

"I don't think he likes it when anyone else plays with his toy," said Charlie.

"Let's try a different one." Meg rolled a little ball with a bell in it across the floor.

Tiger leaped happily after it, but Velvet just huddled inside his carrier.

"I don't think he's used to being around other cats," Charlie said thoughtfully. "He has his own bedroom at Miss Penigree's. I bet Velvet would like a quiet room to himself."

"Like Matilda, when she was having her kittens," Meg remembered. "We put her next door, in the box room."

"Great idea!" Charlie closed the carrier while Meg picked up Velvet's bag. They went out to the hallway.

"It will be nice and quiet in here, Velvet," Charlie announced, throwing open the box room door.

"Neeeigh!"

Meg's and Charlie's mouths dropped open. At the back of the storage room, surrounded by animal carriers and boxes, was a white pony no bigger than a Labrador. He stood next to a trough of oats and a big bowl of water.

"Neeeigh!" The tiny pony trotted quietly up to them. There was something strange about his hooves — they didn't *clip-clop* on the wooden floor.

Meg gasped. "He's wearing SNEAKERS!"

The miniature pony nuzzled Velvet's carrier.

"We can't scare Velvet!" Charlie pulled the carrier away and hurriedly closed the door.

The twins could hardly believe what they had seen.

What was a mini, sneaker-wearing pony doing at Pet Hotel?

The twins hurried downstairs to their family's kitchen. Mom, Dad, and Saffron were sitting around the table. A gerbil cage with a heavy padlock on the door was on the floor by Dad's feet. In the corner of the cage, Pinto snoozed in a cozy nest of shredded paper.

Buster was lying across Saffron's sandals. He bounded over when he saw Meg.

"Why is there a pony in the box room?" Charlie asked, setting Velvet's carrier down on a chair.

"That's Chance," Mom explained, clutching her teacup. "He's not just any miniature pony, he's a guide horse for the blind."

"You mean he's like a guide dog?" Meg asked as Buster rolled over on his back so she could tickle his fluffy stomach.

"That's right," Mom said.

"Wow!" the twins exclaimed together.

Saffron clapped her hands in delight. "Isn't it wonderful? He's been trained to meet all sorts of people and animals and not to be spooked by new surroundings. He takes care of his person so well."

"Where is his person?" Charlie asked.

"He had to go to the hospital and have his appendix removed," Mom explained. "Chance arrived while you were out."

"Just as we were dealing with the gerbil crisis." Dad sighed and took a sip of his tea. "We put Chance in the box room while we tracked them all down."

"Why is he wearing sneakers?" Meg asked.

"To keep his hooves from slipping on smooth surfaces," Mom said.

"Chance is very, very smart," Saffron

told them. “He’s even been taught to knock on the door with his little hoof when he needs to go out and do his pony business.”

Charlie and Meg laughed.

“We were just talking about him,” said Dad. “He seems lonely without his human.” He put his cup down and got to his feet. “I’ll get Chance out of the box room now and find him some company.”

“Can Velvet can stay in the box room instead?” Charlie asked, pointing to the cat carrier.

"We think he'd prefer a room to himself," Meg explained. "He doesn't like the other cats."

"Sure," Mom agreed. "In all the excitement, I almost forgot about him." She peeked into the carrier. "He's very beautiful!"

"He's a Persian show cat," Charlie informed them. "Miss Penigree says we have to keep him clean and ready for the Celebrity Pet Show!"

There was a small meow from the cat carrier. Buster leaped to his feet and ran up to it, wagging his tail.

"Snuuurf!" He sniffed curiously at the carrier.

"Yeeow!" Velvet meowed in alarm and Buster backed away.

"Oh, dear." Charlie sighed. "Velvet doesn't like puppies much, either."

"Poor Velvet. The only thing he likes is his ribbon toy." Meg rummaged in Velvet's bag for the tassel, but it wasn't there. "I must have left it in the Egyptian room," she said. "I'll go get it."

Meg raced up the stairs and dashed into the cat room. Through the bars of Tiger's pen, she could see the big ginger cat and Woody playing, rolling over and over in a tangle of black-and-white and ginger tails and paws. The cat and the kitten were having such a great time that Meg couldn't help giggling.

At the sound of Meg's laughter, Woody and Tiger stopped rolling and slowly got to their feet. They looked guilty.

"Oh, no!" Meg groaned.

Caught in the bars of Tiger's pen was Velvet's favorite toy. It was in tatters. Meg picked up the pieces of soggy shredded ribbon. There was no way she could put the toy back together. Tiger and Woody had totally destroyed it!

Charlie appeared at the door, holding Velvet's carrier. "Why are you taking so long?" he asked.

"Woody and Tiger ruined Velvet's toy," Meg whispered. "Don't let him see!" She stuffed the tattered bits of ribbon into the trash and hurried out to the hallway. Woody darted out with her as she closed the door.

"Velvet can have one of Woody's toys to replace it," Charlie said. "Woody has so many, I'm sure he won't mind."

He led the way to his bedroom, Woody scampering behind them. Charlie lifted Velvet out of the carrier and set him on the paw-print duvet cover. Velvet looked up hopefully.

Meg laughed. "He's expecting you to hand him his toy, like Miss Penigree's butler did!"

Charlie grabbed a feather on a string.

"Here you are, Master Velvet!" he joked, swinging the feather in front of Velvet's nose. "Master Woody loves this. . . ."

Woody jumped onto the bed and tried to bat the feather, but Velvet just sat there, blinking.

"Let's try the laser pointer." Meg picked up a small metal tube the size of a fat pencil, and clicked it on. As she shone it on the walls, a narrow beam of red light danced across the pictures of jungle animals. Woody threw himself into the air, batting at the dot of light, but Velvet just stared around the room.

"He's not interested," Charlie said with a shrug.

Velvet hopped off the bed and stalked off, uttering sad little meows as he peered in the corners and behind the curtains. *"Meow, meow, meow!"*

"He must be looking for his ribbon toy," Meg said as Velvet disappeared under Charlie's bed.

"Come on out, Velvet, it's dusty under there!" Charlie laid on his stomach and pulled Velvet out. Charlie's T-shirt and the ends of Velvet's long fur were covered in fluff. Charlie tried wiping it off with his hand, but all he did was rub the dust into Velvet's fur. Velvet looked as if he'd turned gray.

"The dust will come off when we brush him," Meg said reassuringly. "The important thing is to find him something to play with."

Charlie thought for a moment. “Saffron’s feather boas!” he exclaimed. “All the animals love them. She said we could go get them whenever we wanted” He picked up Velvet and they headed for Saffron’s room.

The vivid turquoise and pink wall hangings fluttered as they opened the door. By the window, crystal wind chimes tinkled and twinkled. Meg pulled out a wicker tray from under the bed and, one by one, shook Saffron's brightly colored boas in front of Velvet's nose. Tufts of blue, orange, green, and silver feathers floated down and settled on Velvet's dusty white fur, but he didn't even blink.

"There must be *something* he wants to play with," Meg said.

"Woody loves to bat the leaves of the potted palm on the landing." Charlie carried Velvet out of Saffron's room and set him down next to the big brass pot. Then he pulled a leaf and let it go, so that it moved up and down. Velvet's eyes opened wide as Charlie wiggled it with his hand.

"He likes it," Charlie whispered as Velvet sprang up.

Thump! Velvet jumped into the plant and began scratching at the damp soil. Bits of dirt flew up and stuck in his fur. Velvet squatted and made a little puddle.

Meg gasped. "He thinks it's a fancy litter box!"

Charlie lifted Velvet out. The dusty white Persian looked as if he were wearing muddy socks. Charlie groaned. "Now his feet are dirty, too."

Suddenly, a volley of barks echoed through the hotel. The noise was coming from Reception.

"That's Buster! What's going on?" Meg rushed downstairs, closely followed by Charlie, who was still clutching Velvet.

Dad, Buster, and Chance were in the entrance hall.

"Woof! Woof! Woof!" Buster barked excitedly as he danced around the tiny horse.

Chance tossed his head and stomped his tiny sneakers.

"I figured Chance would like to lead someone around, like he leads his person," Dad explained. "But Buster thinks it's a game!"

"Shhh, Buster," Meg soothed her puppy. "You'll upset Velvet."

PET HOTEL

"Meeeooowww!" Velvet yowled.

"Too late." Charlie groaned.

"We'd love to play with Chance," Meg told Dad, "but we have to find something to cheer up Velvet first!"

"Let's try the basement," Charlie suggested. "Woody's fascinated by the fish. Maybe Velvet will be, too."

The old swimming pool in the basement was now home to big orange goldfish that swam lazily through the water. Bright green lily pads with pastel-pink water lilies dotted the surface.

Velvet pricked up his ears and stared at the fish.

"He's definitely interested!" Charlie exclaimed, putting Velvet down.

Velvet sat on the edge of the pool and stretched out a dainty paw. He batted a lily pad. A fish that had been hiding underneath it shot off.

The big, fluffy Persian cat threw himself into the air — and pounced into the water!

SPLASH! Velvet spluttered, his paws paddling wildly.

"He's sinking!" Charlie yelled. "Velvet can't swim!"

"I'll get him!" Meg leaned over, grabbed Velvet around his middle, and hauled him out. He was covered in smelly weeds and drops of greenish water.

"Meeeow!" Velvet cried sadly. The whiskers by his stubby little nose quivered.

Charlie raced for a towel. "Sorry, Velvet," he murmured, wrapping up the dripping-wet cat. "We were only trying to make you happy."

Meg shook her head. "He's the first guest who hasn't enjoyed staying at Pet Hotel." She frowned. "Poor Velvet, his fur is filthy. What would Miss Penigree say if she could see him now?"

"There's only one thing we can do," Charlie declared. "Give Velvet a bath!"

He carried the wriggling, damp, and dirty Persian cat up to Reception. Velvet yowled and yowled.

"I'll get his grooming equipment." Meg raced into the kitchen to grab Velvet's bag while Charlie pressed the elevator button to take them up to the bathroom on the third floor.

When the elevator doors opened, Dad and Chance were inside. All the twins could see of Chance was his rear end. The mini-horse's nose was pressed against the back of the elevator.

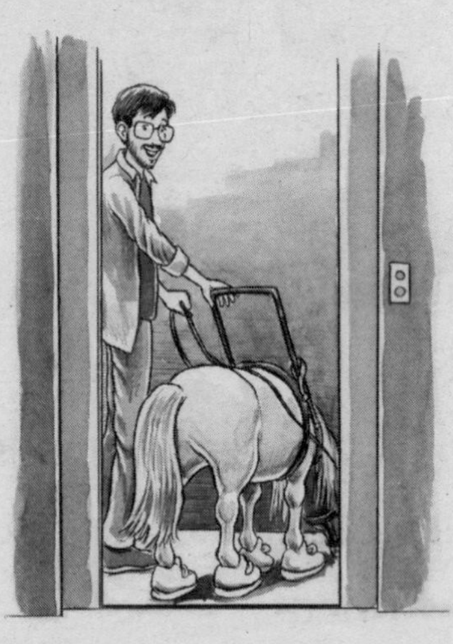

"Chance likes leading people into elevators!" Dad told them, raising his voice above Velvet's cries. "He must be very helpful when his human goes shopping in a big store."

"He isn't bothered by Velvet's noise,"

Meg remarked, patting the rump of the placid little horse.

Chance shuffled his sneakers and flicked his silky white tail from side to side.

Velvet stopped yowling and stared.

"Meeow!" Velvet squirmed out of Charlie's arms, shot into the elevator, and swiped at Chance's tail with a grubby paw.

Chance gave a friendly neigh and flicked his tail again. Velvet batted at it delightedly.

The twins could hardly believe their eyes.

"Velvet's finally found something he likes!" Charlie said, breathing a sigh of relief.

Meg giggled. "It must be because Chance's tail looks just like Velvet's favorite toy."

"Chance seems to like Velvet playing with his tail," said Dad, laughing. "Maybe he and Velvet are the perfect playmates!"

Charlie set Velvet down on the bathroom's black-and-white tiles as Meg ran water into the old enamel tub. It had iron feet shaped like a lion's paws.

Meg took out Velvet's grooming things and lined them up on the windowsill. "Kitty shampoo, kitty comb, kitty brush . . ."

Charlie leaned over the tub and stuck his elbow into the shallow water. "My book about pets says you should always test the temperature of the water with your elbow, because your hands can tolerate water that's too hot," he explained.

"Time to make you beautiful again, Velvet," Meg crooned, picking up the smelly Persian cat.

Velvet stared at the bath.

"Yeoooooooowl!" he squalled. He leaped into the air and rocketed out of the bathroom.

The twins raced after him and managed to corner the cat at the end of the hallway. He was shaking.

"Poor thing," Meg murmured. "How can we calm him down?"

"I've got an idea," Charlie told her. He

ran downstairs. Dad was in the kitchen, feeding Chance an apple.

"We need Chance's help with Velvet!" he panted.

"Go ahead." Dad grinned. "Helping is what he's trained to do."

Charlie grabbed the harness on Chance's back. The miniature guide horse put his ears back to listen for his command.

"To the elevator," Charlie told Chance. The tiny horse trotted to the elevator and waited

patiently for the door to open. Charlie led him in and pressed the button for the top floor.

"Back up!" Charlie ordered when the doors opened again. Chance backed out of the elevator and walked backward down the hallway, carefully placing each little horsey sneaker.

"That's amazing!" Meg murmured. Velvet's eyes opened wide as he watched Charlie and Chance come closer. His whiskers quivered.

"Stop!" Charlie said. "You're a good boy, Chance!"

Chance halted in front of Velvet and swished his long white tail.

Velvet stopped shaking. He stretched out a dirty paw.

"It's working!" Meg sighed with relief as Velvet batted the tiny horse's silky tail. "Walk on, Chance!" Charlie commanded.

Chance slowly led the way to the bathroom. Velvet followed, batting Chance's tail all the way.

"Chance is so well trained!" Meg declared as she helped Charlie maneuver the miniature guide horse so that his tail was hanging over the bathtub. Velvet leaped up to bat it — and landed in the water with a splash!

He looked around in alarm.

"Uh-oh." Charlie groaned.

"Neeeigh!" Chance gave a comforting whinny and flicked his tail.

Velvet blinked and focused on Chance's silky white tail. He reached up a paw to bat at it again.

"Nice job, Chance. Nice job, Velvet," Meg murmured soothingly as she worked the shampoo into Velvet's fur.

Velvet began to purr.

"He must be used to being shampooed," Meg told Charlie.

Soon, Velvet was clean again. Charlie lifted him out of the bathtub and wrapped him in a towel, being careful to keep him close to Chance's tail.

Mom poked her head around the bathroom door. "How are you doing?"

"Fine — but I'm not sure about the bathtub." Meg wiped a handful of fur off the enamel.

"Hmmm," said Mom thoughtfully. "It would be nice to have a separate place to bathe our guests. I'll clean up in here. You take Chance and Velvet to the box room so Velvet can dry off."

Meg and Charlie led Chance, and Chance

led Velvet, to the elevator and down to the box room on the floor below.

"Velvet loves Chance's tail." Charlie chuckled as they crowded into the small room.

Meg laughed. "And Chance loves leading Velvet around. It's a great partnership!"

Velvet played happily with Chance's tail while Charlie retrieved Velvet's carrier and bag and Meg grabbed a litter box and kitty bowls from the Egyptian room. She put them down next to Chance's water bowl and trough of oats.

Charlie opened a can of Perfect Paws cat food and scooped it into a bowl. Velvet nibbled at it daintily. Chance stood next to him and took a mouthful of oats. Soon, the box room rumbled with contented purrs and chomping noises.

Meg and Charlie breathed a sigh of relief. They'd done it! Velvet and Chance were happy together in the box room — and Velvet was clean again, even if it was going to take his fur hours to dry. Velvet's visit to Pet Hotel was going to work out after all!

"Can you take the dogs and Chance out to the park to do their business?" Dad called up the stairs. "Better be quick. The weather report says there's a storm on its way."

Charlie and Meg jumped to their feet.

"We'll bring Chance back soon," Charlie promised Velvet as he pulled the door closed and headed for the elevator.

"I'll get the doggie guests and Buster." Meg raced to the forest room.

Soon, Toby the Great Dane, Sausage the dachshund, Bramble the old black Labrador, Daisy the Westie, and Buster were all leashed up and ready to go. Charlie grabbed Chance's harness in one hand and Toby's leash in the other, while Meg took charge of Buster and the remaining dogs.

Chance strode ahead as they went out into Gazebo Square.

"He's used to being in front," Charlie remarked. The sky was overcast, and the market was crowded with people hurrying to buy things before it rained. There were so many people around Carmen's cupcake stall that they couldn't even see her. At Cocina Mexicana, Juan was dishing out taco dinners as fast as he could.

"Hey, Juan!" Charlie called.

Juan's eyes nearly popped out of his head. "That dog is bigger than the horse!" he said with a laugh, pointing to Toby and Chance.

Paco, Juan's puppy, barked in amazement. *"Woof! Woof! Woof!"*

People turned to stare. Chance walked on, calmly.

A girl with a cloud of dark hair waved and hurried toward them, clutching a bag. It was Polly, the twins' new friend. They'd met her after one of her pigeons strayed into Pet Hotel.

"Hi, Polly. This is Chance, the miniature guide horse," Meg said proudly. "He's staying with us. Chance, meet Polly!" Chance held out a little hoof for Polly to shake.

"He's so cool," Polly murmured, shaking Chance's hoof. She scratched his ears. "Can

I give him a carrot? I just bought a bag of vegetables for Mom to make soup."

Polly looked down as she rummaged in the bag. Then her mouth opened in surprise and she pointed at Chance's tail. "Hey," she said, "who's this?"

Meg and Charlie turned to look. It was a very damp white Persian cat. Chance flicked his tail so that his friend could play with it.

"Velvet!" Charlie groaned. "I thought I'd closed the box room door."

"He must have snuck out to follow Chance," said Meg with a sigh. "A busy market is no place for a show cat — and we just got him clean."

"I'll take him back to the hotel." Charlie handed Chance's harness to Polly and Toby's leash to Meg. But before he could scoop up Velvet, there was a sudden clap of thunder.

CRAAACK!

"Yeeeow!" screeched Velvet. He turned and darted back toward Pet Hotel as the skies opened and rain came down in buckets.

The light on the crosswalk signal turned red.

"Cars are coming!" Meg shouted helplessly, trying to turn the tangle of dogs. "He'll get run over!"

Charlie raced toward Velvet. The terrified cat was heading right into the path of an oncoming car!

"Neeeeeigh!" Chance whinnied, pulling his harness out of Polly's grasp.

Meg held her breath as Chance galloped past Velvet and skidded to a halt, blocking the cat from the road. The car whizzed past, spraying them both with dirty water.

Charlie rushed up. Velvet was once again filthy, wet, and trembling. But he was okay!

"Neeeigh," Chance whinnied softly, nuzzling Velvet. The cat gave a loud *"meeow!"* and batted at the pony's tail.

"Great job, Chance! You saved Velvet!" Charlie said. He took hold of Chance's harness as Meg and the dogs caught up with them.

The miniature guide horse led Charlie, Meg, Velvet, and the dogs to the nearest

crosswalk and waited until the lights changed.

"Chance is a TERRIFIC guide horse!" Meg declared as he took them all safely across the street and back into Pet Hotel.

Mom opened the door and they all trooped inside, dripping.

"We had to bring Velvet back, so we didn't get as far as the park." Meg grimaced. "He needs another bath, I'm afraid."

"Come with me!" Mom led them down to the basement. Chance stepped slowly and carefully down the stairs, followed closely by Velvet and the dogs.

“Ta-da!” Mom opened the door to the laundry room. At one end she’d set up a big tub with fancy pet shampoos, sponges, brushes — and a hair dryer!

Mom smiled. “Welcome to the pet spa.” She began to fill the tub with warm water from the sink.

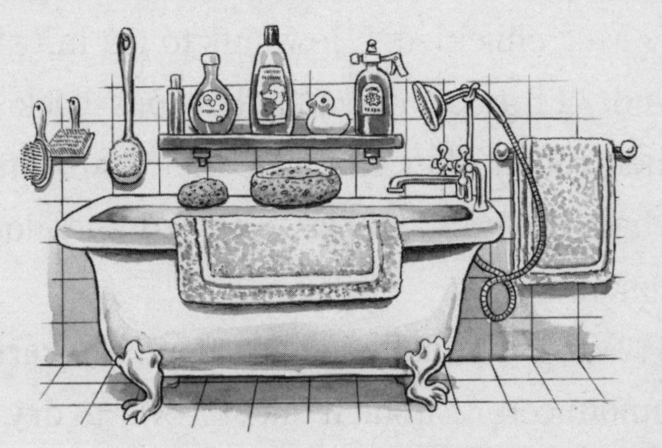

Charlie picked up a bottle of purple shampoo. “Calming lavender,” he read. “That’s just what Velvet needs!”

Chance stood with his tail over the edge of the tub as Charlie gently lowered Velvet into the water. Meg brushed Chance while Charlie washed Velvet and Mom toweled off the dogs.

"Woof!" barked Buster, wagging his tail and putting his front legs up on the tub.

Meg chuckled. "He wants to get in," she said. "I'll take him and the dogs back to their room. They can have their walk later, when the rain stops." She led the dogs upstairs.

"Velvet's finally clean again," Charlie announced. "But he'll take forever to dry."

Mom held up the hair dryer. "Not if you use this. . . ."

Velvet squirmed in alarm as Mom switched it on and handed it to Charlie.

"Neigh!" whinnied Chance comfortingly, nuzzling at Velvet. Soon, the cat was purring as the warm air ruffled his fur and silky tail.

"Good as new," Mom declared.

"Velvet looks amazing!" said Meg when she returned. "He's ready for the Celebrity Pet Show!"

The next day, Miss Penigree's limo came back to collect them.

"I hope she won't notice that we had to

bathe Velvet twice — and blow-dry him," Meg muttered as they pulled up to the film star's apartment.

The driver held the door open and they all jumped out.

When the elevator doors opened at the thirty-third floor, Miss Penigree was waiting.

"Velvet, darling!" she exclaimed, rushing to lift the cat out of his carrier. She examined him closely. "You're so handsome!" she crooned. "And so clean. You'll be the star of the show!"

She looked up at Meg, Charlie, Saffron — and Chance.

"What on earth is that pony doing in my elevator?" she demanded. "And why is he wearing sneakers!"

"Chance is a miniature guide horse," Charlie explained.

"He's staying at Pet Hotel with us," Meg added.

"Chance and Velvet have become such good friends, they like to go everywhere together," Saffron continued as Chance trotted out of the elevator.

"Meeeeow!" Velvet squirmed out of Miss Penigree's arms and batted at Chance's tail.

Miss Penigree's eyes widened.

Saffron began, "Well, I'm really sorry, but Velvet's toy was destroyed . . ."

"...but Chance's tail made a great replacement," Meg finished hurriedly.

"And it comes attached to a friend!" Charlie added.

There was a long pause. Then Miss Penigree gave a tinkling laugh.

"How clever!" she said. "Velvet is such a terror when he loses his toy — that's why I have a whole drawer full of spares."

Miss Penigree pulled open a drawer in the hall side table and took out a tassel toy exactly like the one Woody and Tiger had ruined.

"Meow!" Velvet meowed happily and made a lunge for it.

"My dears, it's time we were going," Saffron told the twins.

Charlie gently pulled Chance's harness. The pony whinnied as they turned to leave. *"Neeeigh!"*

Velvet dropped his toy and raced toward him. Chance lowered his head and nuzzled Velvet's ears. Velvet purred and put out his paw to gently touch Chance's nose.

Miss Penigree wiped a tear from her eye. "My goodness. Velvet ADORES Chance! I do hope Chance's owner will bring him to visit. I could send my limo."

"I'm sure he will, when he hears how much Chance likes Velvet," Meg assured her.

Charlie, Meg, Saffron, and Chance all stepped into the elevator.

Miss Penigree waved good-bye. "You did a wonderful job of taking care of Velvet," she called as the doors began to close. "I'll be sure to tell everyone at the Celebrity Pet Show about your excellent Pet Hotel!"

Check out who's checking in —
see how it all started in the first
Pet Hotel book!

Pet Hotel #1: Calling All Pets!

WELCOME TO GAZEBO SQUARE!

Eight-year-old twins Charlie and Meg beamed as they read the sign. The street was bustling with brightly colored tents and happy, smiling people.

"I can't believe we're really going to live here!" Charlie exclaimed, hoisting up his heavy backpack.

Meg sniffed the air. "Yum!" she murmured. "Chocolate and spices and flowers . . ."

Dad heaved an enormous suitcase down the last step from the train station and paused to catch his breath. "This is a very special place," he said with a grin. "The farmers' market is open every day. Gazebo Square makes everyone feel at home."

"You're going to love Great-Great-Aunt Saffron's hotel!" Mom added.

"I hope we love Great-Great-Aunt Saffron," Charlie whispered to Meg. "She must be very, very old."

Meg nodded. Mom and Dad were going to run the hotel so their great-great-aunt didn't have to move to a retirement home.

"Follow me!" Mom called over her shoulder. They set off through the rainbow maze of tents. There were fruit and vegetable stands, cheese and milk stands, even a cupcake stand! The twins gazed around in eye-popping wonder. Gazebo Square was awfully different from their old home in the country!

Mom paused by a circular, open-air hut where a band was playing cheerful calypso music on steel drums.

“This is the gazebo the square was named after,” she announced.

“Cool!” Meg and Charlie said together.

“See the old archway that the workmen are fixing?” Mom said, pointing to the nearby entrance to the square. “That leads to a park with trees and a pond!”

“Are there any animals there?” Charlie asked hopefully. “I haven’t seen any yet. . . .”

But before Mom could answer, a bundle of yellow fur raced out from under a tent. It was heading straight for them! Meg dropped her heavy bag in surprise.

It was a golden retriever puppy. He had soft, floppy ears, a damp nose, and a wagging tail. He held a bone-shaped cookie in his mouth, but only for a second. Then the puppy gobbled it up, licked his lips, and gazed at Charlie and Meg with big, dark eyes.

"Paco!" a deep voice called.

The twins looked up. The voice belonged to a tall man with thick, curly hair. He wore a red-and-green T-shirt with *Hecho en Mexico* on the front.

"*Lo siento*, sorry . . ." The man handed Meg her bag and grabbed Paco's trailing leash. "He's been raiding the Pet Bakery on Park Street again! My little puppy's a big handful," he told them with a friendly grin.

"Paco's very cute!" Meg said, tickling the puppy under his furry chin. "I love dogs."

Charlie stroked Paco's back. "I wish we had a cat!" he sighed. Paco pricked up his ears and wagged his tail. "Or a puppy," Charlie added with a laugh.

The man looked at the family's luggage. "Moving in?" he asked.

"Yes, to Diamond Hotel," Mom told him.

"Welcome, neighbors!" the man exclaimed. "I run Cocina Mexicana." He pointed to his stall. "My name's Juan. Come and see me when you're hungry!"

They promised that they would, and waved good-bye. As they walked along Gazebo Square, Charlie daydreamed about their new home.

"Diamond Hotel," he murmured. "It

sounds like somewhere movie stars would stay."

"It might be like a palace!" Meg whispered to her brother, eyes shining.

Mom had stopped in front of a tall brownstone. It was covered in crumbly plaster that might once have been brown but now looked almost black. Over the battered door was a wooden sign that read THE DIAMOND HOTEL.

The twins' mouths dropped open.

"It's called that because Diamond is Saffron's last name," Mom explained, raising her voice as one of the workmen at the archway nearby turned on a big drill. The vibrations made the ground rumble. Bits of plaster fell off the front of Diamond Hotel and dust showered down on the twins' heads.

Plunk! The hotel sign landed with a *thud* at their feet.

Meg and Charlie looked at each other. What would Diamond Hotel be like inside?

Dad rapped on the rickety wooden door, but there was no answer.

"Maybe it's unlocked." Meg turned the handle, and the door slowly creaked open.

The twins stepped into a dim hall jam-packed with boxes, coats, shoes, and umbrellas. Everything was covered in a thick layer of dust. It rose in a cloud as they dropped their luggage on the moth-eaten carpet.

Mom took one look inside and clapped her hand to her mouth.

Dad flicked a light switch.

"Not working," he said, coughing.

"Aunt Saffron," Mom called. "We're here!"

There was no reply. Where could Aunt Saffron be?

* * *

Dad picked his way across the room to the front desk. “There’s a reservation book,” he murmured. Charlie and Meg crowded around as Dad brushed off the dust. The open pages were blank, except for the name of one guest. . . .

“Mrs. Ponsonby,” they read together.

“That’s today’s date!” Dad exclaimed. “It looks like she’s due to arrive any minute.”

Just then, there was a knock on the door.

Meg rushed to open it. Standing on the doorstep was a woman in a bright-pink suit. By her side, on a leash, was a tiny poodle with a glittery silver collar.

As Meg opened her mouth to greet them, Mrs. Ponsonby stepped past her into the hall. “Dear me!” she said, looking around in disgust.

Her poodle trotted after her and snuffled at the coat stand. It wagged its tail.

“This is a run-down dump!” the woman declared. “We can’t spend the night in a place like this. Come on, Petal! We’re leaving!”

She swept out, dragging the curious poodle behind her.

“I think Petal wanted to stay!” Charlie snickered.

Mom was looking worried. “How will we keep this place going if we don’t have any guests?” she said under her breath. “And where in the world is Saffron?”

WHERE EVERY PUPPY FINDS A HOME

Meet GERONIMO STILTONOO

He is a cavemouse — Geronimo Stilton's ancient ancestor! He runs the stone newspaper in the prehistoric village of Old Mouse City. From dealing with dinosaurs to dodging meteorites, his life in the Stone Age is full of adventure!

#1 The Stone of Fire

#2 Watch Your Tail!

#3 Help, I'm in Hot Lava!

#4 The Fast ar the Frozen